## THIS BOOK
## BELONGS TO

This edition published by HarperCollins Publishers Ltd 1996
First published 1950 by Sampson Lowe
© Darrell Waters Limited 1950 as to all text and illustrations
Enid Blyton's signature mark and the word 'NODDY' are Registered
Trade Marks of Enid Blyton Ltd
ISBN 0 00 198232-X
Printed and bound in Italy

# HURRAH FOR LITTLE NODDY

BY Enid Blyton

## CONTENTS

Collins

*A Division of* HarperCollins*Publishers*

EVERYONE HAD TO LINE UP AND PUT ONE LARGE BROWN
PENNY INTO ONE OF THE POLICEMEN'S HELMETS

1

## HOUSE-FOR-ONE

"MILKO! Milko!" shouted a voice just outside Tubby Cottage. Mr Tubby the teddy bear lived there, and his fat little wife put her head out of the window.

"Two bottles, please," she called. "And oh, milkman, you'd better call at the house next door – the little new one, called House-for-One. Mr Noddy lives there, and he may want some milk. He's just come."

"That house wasn't there yesterday when I came round with the milk," said the little wooden milkman in surprise.

"No, it wasn't. Mr Noddy only came yester-day," said Mrs Tubby. "He and Big-Ears the brownie built it with toy bricks. It's nice, isn't it?"

"I'll go and see if he wants any milk," said the milkman, and he went off with his little cart.

"Milko! Milko!" he called just outside Noddy's window. The little nodding man was asleep, but he woke up with a jump and went to the door, his head nid-nodding madly.

"Good morning," he said. "Yes, I would like some milk."

"One bottle? Two bottles?" asked the wooden milkman. Noddy nodded hard.

"Well, say which you want," said the milkman.

"You nod for one bottle, and you nod for two! How am I to know which you want?"

"ONE BOTTLE? TWO BOTTLES?" ASKED THE WOODEN MILKMAN

"Oh, don't take any notice of my nodding head," said Noddy. "I'm made like that. Look, my head is fixed on my neck on a kind of spring – and if you tap me, I nod very hard indeed!"

"Do let me tap you then," said the milkman, and he tapped Noddy's head smartly. At once his head began to nod up and down very fast indeed. The milkman laughed.

He gave Noddy a bottle of milk. "One penny, please," he said.

"Oh goodness – I forgot. I haven't any money," said Noddy, in dismay.

"Well, you can pay me by letting me tap your head each morning till you've got some money," said the milkman, with a grin. "I'd like that!"

Noddy went indoors with his milk. He had no furniture at all except for a chair that Mr Tubby had lent him to sleep in. Dear, dear – he really must get a job and earn some money! Then he could buy a jug for his milk, a bed to sleep in at night, a carpet for the floor – and lots of other things, too.

Mrs Tubby arrived with a boiled egg and some bread and butter on a plate. "You're a very kind teddy indeed," said Noddy. "I'd like to give you a hug only my body is made of wood and I might hurt you. I do wish I knew how to get some work to do. Do you know anyone who wants a very willing workman, Mrs Tubby?"

11

"Well, you might go and try at Four-Chimney House," said Mrs Tubby. "They're spring-cleaning, you know. It's quite a big doll's house. If you can scrub and polish I should think they'd pay you well."

"I'll go this very morning," said Noddy, happily. "Isn't the house I built lovely, Mrs Tubby? I do feel proud of it. I'm so pleased to be living in Toyland. People seem so nice here."

"Oh, we're not *all* nice," said Mrs Tubby. "You've got to be careful of one or two of the monkeys – and be sure you don't get in the way of the clockwork doll who goes head-over-heels. He gets in *such* a temper if you do!"

"I'll be very careful," said Noddy. "Now I'm off to look for work!"

## 2

## NODDY GOES TO WORK

THE little nodding man put on his pointed hat with the jingling bell at the top. He rubbed his shoes with a bit of paper, because he hadn't even a shoe-brush. Then he set off to find Four-Chimney House.

It was quite easy to find because it was the only house with four chimneys. It was a very nice doll's house, with a garage at the side, and a flower garden at the front. A little blue car was in the garage.

Noddy went round to the back door. A small doll in a big white apron opened the door. She had curly golden hair and bright blue eyes. She looked at Noddy, and he bowed, his head nodding all the time.

"What do you want?" she said. "Are you the laundry, or the chimney-sweep?"

"No, I'm only Noddy," said Noddy. "I heard you were spring-cleaning. I'm sure I would be good at that, because I've got plenty of spring in me, and I'm full of leaps and bounds."

"That's nothing to do with spring-cleaning," said the little doll. "We're cleaning the house because it's *springtime*, silly. Come in. I'll see if I can find something for you to do."

The little doll thought for a moment. "The sweep hasn't come," she said. "I suppose you don't know how to sweep chimneys, do you?"

"I'm sure I *could* sweep your four chimneys," said Noddy, at once. "I'll try."

So he was set to work to sweep the chimneys.

14

THE LITTLE DOLL-CHILDREN RAN OUTSIDE SO THEY COULD
TELL HIM WHEN THE BRUSH CAME OUT AT THE TOP

He poked the brush up each chimney, and the little doll-children ran outside so that they could tell him when the brush came out at the top.

"You've done very well," said the golden-haired doll, when he had swept all the chimneys. "Your face is very dirty now. Go and wash in the sink."

So Noddy went to the kitchen sink and washed himself. Then he was set to work to scrub the big kitchen floor. He did it so well that everyone came to see how nice it was. "You're a very good worker," said the doll. "Now will you please carry some rubbish out to the bottom of the back garden for me, and put it on the bonfire to burn? Can you make a bonfire?"

"Oh *yes*," said Noddy. "I've never made one before, but I'd love to."

16

Well, he was given all sorts of things to take down to the bonfire. He was given an old bed, a broken chair, a table whose top was cracked, and a carpet with holes in it. Noddy didn't put them on the bonfire. He stood and looked at them all lying in a heap where he had tipped them out of his barrow.

"Why, I could mend that bed and sleep on it," he thought. "And that chair would just fit me. And that table would look so nice in my little house if I mended it and painted it! And that carpet just wants patching and it would be so bright and cosy on my floor!"

He ran to ask the golden-haired doll if he could have the things for himself instead of burning them.

"You see, I've a little house—but no furniture at all!" he said. "Your rubbish would do nicely for me till I get some money to buy things."

"Would you really like all that old stuff?" said the golden-haired doll, in surprise.

Noddy nodded like anything. "Oh yes, yes! It would be just right for me."

So that night Noddy piled heaps and heaps of old things on his barrow, and wheeled them to House-for-One. He called out to fat Mr Tubby as he passed.

"A bed to sleep in, a chair to sit on, a table to eat off, a carpet to walk on! A plate and a cup and a dish! An old knife and fork and spoon! A little cracked wash basin! I'm the happiest fellow in the world, Mr Tubby!"

3

## ANOTHER JOB FOR NODDY

NODDY spent a happy evening mending all the things he had been given. You should have seen how different his little house looked with a bit of furniture in it! Noddy lay down on the bed, he sat on the chair, and he ate some supper off the table. He wished Big-Ears the brownie were there to see him.

He had been paid some money for his work that day. He bought his supper and his breakfast out of it, and the rest he put away to give Big-Ears.

"He lent me such a lot of money," thought Noddy, nodding his head as he remembered. "People must always pay back what they borrow. I will put some of my pennies into the drawer of the table. Then I can give them to Big-Ears when he comes."

For three days more Noddy worked hard at Four-Chimney House. The golden-haired doll gave him such a lot of things she didn't want. She even gave him old curtains, and *how* nice his windows looked when he put them up. They were red curtains, with stripes, and they looked very cheerful indeed.

More money went into the kitchen drawer. Noddy began to feel quite rich. But after the three days were up the golden-haired doll didn't want him any more.

"Our spring-cleaning is finished," she said. "Why don't you go to the Toy Garage and ask if you can help to clean the cars there?"

"What a good idea!" said Noddy, and he went there to see if he could get a job.

The garage had a toy petrol station, and was really rather grand. Tiny cars drove up for petrol. Others came in for cleaning and polishing. The owner of the garage was a kindly-looking doll called Mr Sparks. He looked at the little nodding man and liked him.

21

"Yes, you can come and clean cars for me," he said. "My man is away. You can have his job till he comes back."

Noddy set to work happily. He liked the bright little cars. They were all colours: red, blue, yellow, green and orange.

"Oh, if only I had a car of my own!" thought Noddy. "Wouldn't that be lovely? But I shall never, never be rich enough to own one. Look at this yellow one—did you ever see such a little beauty?"

He pressed the horn, and it hooted: "Parp, parp, parp!"

Mr Sparks, the garage owner almost jumped out of his skin. "Hey!" he shouted. "You're supposed to clean the cars, not hoot the horns! You get on with your work!"

"Sorry," said Noddy, and he set to work to clean and polish. Soon he could see his face in

HE PRESSED THE HORN AND IT HOOTED:
"PARP, PARP, PARP!"

the bonnet of every single car. Mr Sparks was very pleased.

"Come tomorrow," he said. "And here's your pay. You're a good worker."

"More money!" thought Noddy, pleased, as he hurried home that night. "Half to put away for Big-Ears, and half to spend on myself. What shall I buy for my supper? I'll get a big jammy bun and a big ice-cream. That will be a very nice supper. I'll sit in my own little chair and eat off my own little table."

For a whole week Noddy worked at the Toy Garage. Then the other man came back and Mr Sparks said he wouldn't need him any more. Noddy was very sad.

"Oh dear—now I've got to get another job," he thought. "I must get one quickly, too, or my money will all go."

He went home thinking so hard about it that he left his little hat behind, the one with the bell on top. "Bother!" he said. "I've forgotten my hat. I'll go and fetch it after I've had my supper!"

4

## NODDY IS VERY BRAVE

AFTER he had had his supper that night Noddy set off to fetch his cap from the garage. The moon was up, and sailed in and out of the clouds, so that sometimes it was very dark and sometimes it was very light.

He came to the garage just as the moon sailed out of the clouds—and he saw something that puzzled him very much!

"The garage door is open!" said Noddy, surprised. "Who is there at this time of night?"

Then he heard a noise. "R-r-r-r-r-r! R-r-r-r-r!"

"Well! Someone is going to run a car out of the garage!" thought Noddy. "In the middle of the night! Can it be a thief—someone who has come to steal one of Mr Sparks' cars?"

He stood in the shadows and watched. Out came a car, driven by a little goblin. Then another—and another—and another!

Noddy was so surprised that he couldn't even shout. Why—it wasn't just *one* car that was being stolen—it was all of them!

"There goes the car belonging to the Sailor Doll," thought Noddy, as a little yellow car roared past. "And there's the red one belonging to the three Skittles. And there's the one belonging to the Wobbly Man—and my goodness there's the grand one that's owned by Jumbo the toy elephant! I'd know his anywhere, it's so big!"

Noddy suddenly knew he must do something about this. But what could he do? There were so many

26

ALL THE CARS WERE RACING OUT OF THE GARAGE
AS FAST AS THEY COULD GO!

goblins—one to each car—and all the cars were racing out of the garage as fast as they could go!

Noddy remembered a little old car that stood in a shed nearby. He ran to see if it was there. Yes, it was.

"I'll get in it and drive after the thieves!" thought Noddy, bravely. "I can't fight them, there are too many—but at least I can follow them and see where they go."

He got into the funny little car. He started it. It ran noisily out of the old shed and down the pathway to the road. The last of the goblins' cars was just turning a corner in the distance. The moon was out at that moment and Noddy could see quite well.

28

Off he went. He had never driven a car before, but he didn't mind. He knew how to steer, and although he wobbled a bit, he kept the car on the road. R-r-r-r-r-r! Off went Noddy!

All through Toyland he went, and out into the country. Far away ahead all the other cars raced at sixty miles an hour. Noddy followed, turning corners on two wheels, and yelling at any rabbit that was in his way.

He went quite a long way—and then something dreadful happened!

A wheel came off his car! It was such a very *old* car, and one of the front wheels had always been loose. Now that the car was going at such a speed, off came the wheel! It rolled down the road, scared a peeping rabbit, and ran into a bush. The car spun round on its three wheels, and crashed into a tree.

Noddy flew right up in the air out of the car, the steering-wheel still in his hands. He landed in the middle of a bush, which was very lucky for him.

He lay there, gasping, all his breath knocked out of him. Even his head stopped nodding. Then gradually it began to nod again, and he sat up.

A small, frightened voice called out to him: "What's happened? Who are you?"

Noddy knew that voice. It was the voice of Big-Ears the brownie, his very best friend! Oh, what a bit of luck!

5

## A NIGHT IN THE TOADSTOOL HOUSE

"BIG-EARS!" called Noddy. "Oh Big-Ears! It's me. Noddy, you know. I've had an accident."

Big-Ears the brownie came out into the moon-light, looking scared.

"*Noddy*! I can't believe it. Were you driving a car? In the middle of the night, too. You must be mad."

"No, I'm not mad. I was chasing thieves," said Noddy, standing up and feeling himself all over to see if he was broken anywhere.

"Are you hurt?" asked Big-Ears, anxiously.

"No, I don't think so. I'm a bit chipped *here*," said Noddy, rubbing one shoulder. "And is there a bit off my nose, Big-Ears? Can you see?"

"No, I don't think there is," said Big-Ears.

"Well Noddy, it's nice to see you. Come to my toadstool house. You can sleep there tonight."

Well, that was very nice. Big-Ears' house was most exciting. It was a large toadstool, with a door in the thick stalk, and a tiny stairway going up to the head of the toadstool. There was a queer-shaped room there, very cosy indeed.

"This is nice," said Noddy, his head nodding merrily once more. "Big-Ears, a whole lot of goblins went to Mr Sparks' garage tonight and took every one of the cars there. I followed them as far as here. Then I lost them."

"Oh, *I* know where they are," said Big-Ears at once. "They've gone to Goblin Village, I'm sure. Goblins *love* cars, you know, but they always drive so fast that the police won't let them have any. So I suppose they've stolen those for themselves."

"Well, I never! Then I can go back to Mr Sparks' garage tomorrow and tell him where to look for the cars!" said Noddy, delighted. "Won't he be pleased?"

"Very," said Big-Ears. "Look, here's a hot cup of cocoa and a biscuit. I'll make up a bed for you in my big armchair and you can stay with me tonight. We'll go peeping into

33

Goblin Town tomorrow to see what we can find!"

They had their cups of cocoa and a chocolate biscuit each. Then they climbed into bed and fell fast asleep.

Noddy was very surprised in the morning to find himself in Big-Ears' toadstool house. But he soon remembered everything that had happened. The two talked about it when they ate their breakfast.

"*You'd* better not go to Goblin Village," Big-Ears said to Noddy. "They would wonder why someone from Toyland was there. *I'll* go and peep round. They know me quite well."

So, while Noddy cleaned Big-Ears' little toadstool house for him, Big-Ears went to see what he could find in Goblin Village.

All the goblins were very excited indeed. They

34

ALL THE GOBLINS WERE VERY EXCITED INDEED.
THEY TOOK NO NOTICE OF BIG-EARS

took no notice of Big-Ears. "My car's blue," said one.

"Mine's yellow," said another.

"I got Jumbo's big car," said a third. "Oooh, won't we have fun at nights, racing round the woods!"

"Where are the cars?" said a goblin boy. "I want to see them."

"Well, you can just *peep* at them," said a goblin. "They're down that rabbit-hole by the oak tree, all neatly garaged in a row!"

Well, well—that was all that Big-Ears wanted to know! He shot off at once back to his toadstool house.

"Noddy! Come along. Back to Toy Town we'll go!" he cried. "I know where all the cars are. We'll tell Mr Sparks and the policeman. *How* pleased they'll be!"

He got out his little red bicycle. "Stand on the back," he told Noddy. "Are you ready? Then off we go!"

6

## A SHOCK FOR NODDY

BIG-EARS could pedal very fast indeed on his
bicycle. His feet went up and down like
lightning. He rang his bell loudly all the way.

Everyone skipped out of his path. The rabbits
ran, the mice scurried, the frogs hopped high. The
old toad nearly got run down, but not quite. One
poor worm got run over, but as he wriggled away
quickly down his hole Big-Ears didn't think he
could be hurt very much.

As they got near Toy Town Noddy felt rather
afraid.

"Big-Ears," he said, "I feel scared."

"Why?" asked the brownie in surprise.

"Well—I took that car and smashed it up, you know," said Noddy. "What do you suppose Mr Sparks will say to that? I shouldn't have taken the car, should I? And I certainly shouldn't have smashed it up! Oh dear me!"

"Never mind. They'll get back all their cars because of you," said Big-Ears. "*I* think you were very brave, Noddy."

They rode into Toy Town. What a to-do there was there! Mr Sparks was in a terrible state. All his cars were gone! Yes, even the old one out of the shed!

Jumbo was there, waving his trunk about, very upset that his grand car had been stolen. The three Skittles were looking very angry. The Wobbly Man was wobbling to and fro more than ever, he was so worried.

## A SHOCK FOR NODDY

There were crowds of excited toys all about the market-place, talking about the stolen cars. Mr Plod, the big toy policeman was there, taking notes from Mr Sparks.

Mr Sparks held up Noddy's little pointed hat with its jingling bell.

"I found *this*," he said in a loud voice. "And we all know who *this* belongs to! It's Noddy's—the little nodding man's! What was his hat doing in the garage last night?"

"*He* stole the cars!" cried everyone. "And he dropped his hat by mistake. We must find Noddy."

Big-Ears jumped off his bicycle nearby at that very moment, and the crowd saw Noddy behind him.

"There he is! There he is!" they cried. "Catch him, Mr Plod. Put him in prison!"

And before poor Noddy knew what was happening the policeman had caught hold of him, and with Mr Sparks on the other side, he was marched off to prison!

"He stole the cars!" cried everyone. "What a rogue he is!"

Poor Noddy. He struggled and shouted but it wasn't a bit of good, Mr Sparks and the policeman wouldn't let him go. He looked round for Big-Ears, but the little brownie was quite lost in the crowd.

"I didn't steal the cars, I didn't, I didn't!" cried Noddy. "I came to tell you where they are."

"Ho! You did, did you? Well, of course you know where they

"I DIDN'T STEAL THE CARS, I DIDN'T, I DIDN'T!"
CRIED NODDY

are, if you stole them," said Mr Sparks.

And before poor Noddy could say another word he was shut up in the police-station in a horrid little cell with only one barred window very high

up! How sad he was! His head stopped nodding. He sat down and put it between his hands.

"I'm in prison! I shall be sent right away from Toyland. I shall be punished —and I didn't do anything except go after the thieves," he groaned.

At that moment he heard a tremendous hammering at the door of the police-station. Bang, bang, bang, blim-blam, BANG!

Then he heard a voice. "Let me in! I've got something to say. LET ME IN! I'm Big-Ears the brownie, and I want to tell you all about Noddy, and how brave he's been. LET ME IN, I SAY!"

## 7

## BIG-EARS COMES ALONG

WELL, of course, the policeman had to let Big-Ears in or he would have broken down the door.

"What's all this?" he said, sternly. "Do you want to be put into prison, too?"

"You listen to me, Mr Plod," said Big-Ears, fiercely. "Last night Noddy went back to find his cap because he'd left it in the garage."

"Don't believe it," said Mr Sparks, who was there.

"And he found the garage door open, and there were goblins inside—and they drove your cars out one by one, Mr Sparks. Yes, they did! And Noddy was very brave, he got that old car out of the nearby shed, and drove it full-tilt after them!"

"Good gracious!" said Mr Sparks. "Is this true? Did he really?"

"Yes, he did," went on Big-Ears. "And what's more, we know where the cars are hidden!"

"Where? Tell me where!" cried Mr Sparks; and the policeman looked most excited.

"I shan't tell you," said Big-Ears. "You've been horrid and unkind to my friend Mr Noddy. You've locked him up—that good, kind, brave Noddy."

"Tell us where the cars are, please, please do!" begged Mr Sparks. "We'll set Mr Noddy free, of course we will!"

"No, I *shan't* tell you," said Big-Ears, enjoying himself now. "For one thing poor Noddy had a dreadful accident with that old car. A wheel came off, and the car ran into a tree and broke into bits. I expect you'll be angry with him for that, too. So I shan't tell you where your cars are!"

"Oh, I'll forgive Noddy anything!" said Mr Sparks. "I will, I will. If only I can get the other cars back! That old car was no good. I don't mind its being broken to bits."

"Well *I* think Noddy deserves a reward, not a punishment, for the brave thing he did," said Big-Ears. "I shall tell him not to say a word about where all the cars are unless you give him a fine reward."

45

"Well, I must say I think he *deserves* a reward," said the policeman. "What do you think he would like?"

"Well," said Big-Ears, taking a big breath. "Well—*I* think that as he saved everyone else's cars he ought at least to have a little car of his own—even if it's a very, very little *tiny* one!"

Mr Sparks looked at the policeman, and the policeman looked at Mr Sparks.

"We shouldn't *really* have locked him up without hearing what he had to say," said the policeman.

"He must have been *very* brave to chase those tiresome goblins," said Mr Sparks. He turned to Big-Ears.

"Very well. I will give Noddy a little tiny car of his own, in return for what he did. But now you must tell me where the goblins have hidden the cars."

"Ask Noddy," said Big-Ears. So to Noddy's great surprise, his cell door was opened, and he was taken out very kindly by the policeman and given a big cup of hot coffee and an enormous slice of ginger cake.

46

A BIG CUP OF HOT COFFEE AND AN ENORMOUS SLICE
OF GINGER CAKE

"We beg your pardon for locking you up," said Mr Plod, rather red in the face.

"We want to reward you for your bravery," said Mr Sparks. "Please tell us where the stolen cars are, brave Mr Noddy."

"Well—the goblins hid them down the rabbit-hole by the old oak tree in Goblin Village," said Noddy, his head beginning to nod again. "I'll take you there. I don't really want any reward, though. I'm *dreadfully* sorry for breaking up your old car, Mr Sparks."

"Ah—wait and see what your reward is to be before you say you don't want it!" said Mr Sparks, with a smile.

## 8

## OFF TO GOBLIN VILLAGE!

L OTS of exciting things happened after that.
Mr Plod called six other policemen, and
they all got into a big bus with Mr Sparks, Big-
Ears, the three Skittles, Jumbo the elephant, Mr
Wobbly, the Sailor Doll, three other toys whose
cars had been stolen—and Noddy, of course.

He was next to Jumbo, who squashed him
dreadfully, but Noddy was so pleased at suddenly
being a hero that he really didn't mind. He had
his hat back again, too, and it was nice to hear
its little bell jingling as his head nodded gaily up
and down.

They arrived in Goblin Village. Gobbo, the chief goblin, was called out to see the policemen. He was most alarmed.

"Take me to where you have hidden the stolen cars," commanded Mr Plod.

"We haven't stolen any," said Gobbo, sulkily.

"*Then take me to the rabbit-hole by the old oak tree*," ordered Mr Plod. All the listening goblins howled in fear then, and ran away at top speed. Gobbo was a bit braver than the rest. He went with them to the rabbit-hole—and there were all the cars!

"Just look—all parked nose to tail in a neat row!" said Mr Sparks, amazed. "Gobbo, who stole them?"

50

"JUST LOOK – ALL PARKED NOSE TO TAIL IN A NEAT ROW!"

But Gobbo wouldn't tell.

"Very well—I shall fine every single person in Goblin Village one large round penny," said Mr Plod, firmly. "That will teach them not to go stealing toy cars again!"

And everyone had to line up and put one large brown penny into one of the policemen's helmets. It was very heavy when the last goblin had thrown his penny in!

Then Jumbo got into his car, the three Skittles got into theirs, and the Sailor Doll got into his. Mr Sparks got into his own best car, Mr Wobbly

52

wobbled his way into his—and
soon all the cars had
their right owners at
the steering-wheels.

The policemen, Big-Ears and Noddy went home in the bus. Mr Plod let Noddy drive the bus for a treat, and he was too excited for words.

He drove very carefully indeed, and felt very happy. "I do like driving," he told Big-Ears. "It's a lovely feeling. I do wish I had a car of my own—my very own! But I shall never be rich enough to buy one, shall I, Big-Ears?"

"Never!" said Big-Ears, and smiled a little secret smile all to himself. "What a pity, Noddy, what a pity."

## 9

## THREE CHEERS FOR LITTLE NODDY!

THEY all got back to Toy Town at last—and dear me, whilst they had gone, the news had gone round the town about Noddy's cleverness in chasing the goblins, and finding out where the stolen cars were.

So what do you think? There was a big feast prepared in the market-place for Noddy, Big-Ears, and all their friends! My goodness, you should have seen the jellies shivering in their dishes, the plates of sandwiches, the great big chocolate cakes, the buns and biscuits. It really was a wonderful sight!

"Is this for *us*" said Noddy, in surprise. "Oh my—is this the reward Mr Sparks said I could have? It's lovely!"

"No, no—that isn't the reward you're going to have," said Mr Sparks, gruffly. "Look—there's your reward over there—sitting by itself in the middle of the market-place, Noddy!"

Noddy looked. He saw a car—a very little car, just big enough for two people. It was red and yellow. And it had an enormous blue bow tied to the steering-wheel with a message written on a piece of paper.

"To Noddy. He got back our cars—so now he shall have one for himself!"

Noddy's head nodded so madly that his bell jingled all the time. He couldn't believe his eyes.

"TO NODDY. HE GOT BACK OUR CARS—SO NOW HE
SHALL HAVE ONE FOR HIMSELF!"

"Is it for me? Really for me?" he kept saying. "Oh, I can't believe it! It can't be mine!"

"Well, you come and join the feast—and afterwards you can drive your new car round and round the market-place!" said Mr Sparks. "But we'll have the feast first—just in *case* you run into something and take your appetite away!''

So they all sat down to the feast, and it wasn't long before all the dishes were empty. Mr Tubby the teddy bear called out for three cheers for Mr Noddy, and goodness me, what a noise there was!

And then came the happiest moment of Noddy's day. He got into his own little car! He pressed the hooter. ''Poop-poop,'' it said proudly.

''There's room for a friend,'' said Noddy, looking round. ''Big-Ears, where are you? Come with me on my very first drive in my very own car!''

Big-Ears got in—and off they went at top speed round and round the market-place. ''Poop-poop! Poop-poop! Poop-poop!''

''It's the nicest car in the world,'' said Noddy,

59

delighted. "And OH, Big-Ears! OH, I've got a WONDERFUL idea!"

"What?" asked Big-Ears.

"I'll be a taxi-driver!" said Noddy, happily. "I've got a car—I can take people wherever they want to go. Oh, Big-Ears—isn't that a fine idea? I've got my own job now—I'll drive my taxi!"

It *is* a good idea, little nodding man—and if ever we come to visit Toy Town, we'll ride in your taxi. Are you going to have any more adventures?

Yes, of course you are. We'll read about them all another day!

## THE NODDY LIBRARY